ESMERALDA

AND THE PET PARADE

WITHDRAWN

CECILE SCHOBERLE

SIMON AND SCHUSTER BOOKS FOR YOUNG READERS
Published by Simon & Schuster Inc., New York

This book is illustrated with multicolor linoleum block prints. The text is set in 15pt. Trump Mediaeval.

SIMON AND SCHUSTER BOOKS FOR YOUNG READERS
Simon & Schuster Building, Rockefeller Center, 1230 Avenue of the Americas, New York, New York 10020
Copyright © 1990 by Cecile Schoberle. All rights reserved including the right of reproduction in whole or in part in any form. SIMON AND SCHUSTER BOOKS FOR YOUNG READERS is a trademark of Simon & Schuster Inc. Manufactured in the United States of America.

10 9 8 7 6 5 4 3 2 1

Library of Congress Cataloging-in-Publication Data   Schoberle, Cecile. Esmeralda and the pet parade /
Cecile Schoberle.   p.   cm.
Summary: Juan's rambunctious goat Esmeralda threatens to fulfill his friends' predictions and disrupt the pet parade.   [1. Goats—Fiction.   2. Parades—Fiction.   3. Mexican Americans—Fiction.]   I. Title
PZ7.S3647E5 1990   89-32611
[E]—dc20   CIP AC

ISBN 0-671-67958-9

Dedicated to my parents, Carl and Babs.

rom the beginning,
Esmeralda was always in trouble.

If the flowers were eaten, a trash can knocked over, or Mama's clean laundry pulled down from the line, everyone knew who had done it.

"Esmeraaalda!" Mama would scream. "Juan, come and get that goat of yours!"

"Golly, Essie," Juan would whisper. "Can't you be good?"

On Sunday, Juan's Aunt Bertha came to tea. And on Sunday, Esmeralda decided she liked to roll on the living room rug better than in her bath towel.

On Friday, Juan tried to teach Esmeralda to fetch Papa's slippers. And on Saturday, Mr. Kent, who lived five blocks away, brought them back.

Everyone in the family was against that goat. All except Grandpa. He called her his little explorer. "Columbus, Cortez, Cabeza de Vaca," he said. "The way that goat roams—I tell you, someday she will be famous!"

Grandpa had brought her over from his ranch one morning, all bundled up. When Juan saw that fuzzy white face and those mischievous eyes, he knew he'd found a friend.

That was a year ago. A year full of trouble. But a year full of friendship. When Juan came home from school, Esmeralda was the first to greet him. They did homework together, waded in the creek together, even flew kites together. And if Juan ever needed a friend just to listen, Essie was there.

"Esmeralda," Juan said as he brushed her, "when are you going to grow up and behave? I want Mama and Papa to be as proud of you as I am."

She just smiled and nuzzled his hand. Then she ate the ribbon he'd tied to her horn.

At the neighborhood playground there was magic in the air. It was the week of the Fiesta, the time when the whole city came together to celebrate—with pageants, dancing, and singing. Best of all was the Pet Parade. The children of Santa Fe marched through town with their pets dressed in wild and wonderful costumes. There would be bands playing, crowds cheering, and special prizes for the best-dressed. It was hard to think about anything else.

Juan aimed the ball, then stopped. "How about if I dress Esmeralda as Cinderella? Really show her off."

Lucy grabbed the ball and shot. "Point! Gee, I'm not so sure. I just want one of us on Garcia Street to win first prize."

"Me too," yelled Roberto from his bike. "And Juan...." He looked over at Esmeralda. "Make sure that goat stays in line."

Next day, the gang met in Roberto's backyard.

"Any ideas for our costumes?" asked Roberto.

Carlotta waved brightly colored flags. "We could go as different countries."

"Neat idea!" said Myron. "Who goes as which country?"

"I want to be the U.S.A. And nobody else can," said Roberto.

"Oh, forget it, Roberto," huffed Carlotta.

"How about if we dress our pets as dinosaurs?" said Myron.

"Cool!" exclaimed Lucy. Then she giggled and held up Hamlet, her hamster. "But what kind of monster could this little guy be?" They all rolled with laughter.

"Why don't we choose our own costumes, but all go in the same color?" suggested Carlotta.

"Hmm—you mean, like all dress in blue?" asked Roberto.

"You could put blue paper streamers on your bike, like the floats at the football parade," said Juan excitedly.

"I could decorate my dad's blue fishing hat!" said Myron.

So it was settled. Juan and Myron made plans as they walked home. But as they parted, Myron's last words were, "Juan, don't let your Esmeralda ruin our chances."

Juan was quiet as he and Papa drove over to Grandpa's that evening.

"Something bothering you?" asked Papa. Usually Juan would be excited about a visit to the ranch.

"No, sir," said Juan.

Grandpa greeted Juan at the front door with a hug. "Why this sad face, boy? Come, let's go watch my sunset."

When the evening colors changed day into night, Grandpa could always be found on his back porch. From there, he could watch the stars coming out, and feel the cooling breeze from the distant mountain. It really was Grandpa's sunset, because it was like no other place in the world.

"Grandpa," said Juan slowly, "nobody believes in Esmeralda. They think she wanders, gets into trouble, can't behave. And Grandpa...nobody believes in me."

Watching a lone hawk circle, Grandpa turned to sit by Juan. "You can't change some things, Juanito. Let her be as she is. And remember what I have always told you about your little explorer."

Juan grinned. Grandpa began, "Columbus, Cortez, Cabeza de Vaca. The way that goat roams, I tell you...."

"....someday she will be famous!" Juan chimed in. They laughed and Juan gave Grandpa a big hug.

"Finally! A smile! Now let me show you my newest creation." From pieces of cottonwood and cedar, Grandpa carved beautiful animals and santos. Into Juan's hands he placed a tiny wooden bird.

"Gracias!" called Juan again and again, as Papa backed the truck out of the driveway.

"Remember, Juan," called Grandpa. "It would be easier to change the wild bird in the sky than to change your Esmeralda."

On the day of the Parade Juan awoke with Essie nibbling on his pajama leg. He scrambled into his special blue vest and Fiesta tie, then carefully tied Mama's new blue chiffon scarf around Esmeralda's neck.

"Here's a costume so simple that even you can't mess it up, Esmeralda." He patted her freshly washed head and gave her horns a final polish. Esmeralda smiled up at him.

"I know you'll do your best today, Essie. But, just in case...." Juan reached into a drawer, took out a leash, and clicked it around her neck.

A dog leash! Esmeralda had never worn one before. She balked and pulled. "Come on, Essie," said Juan. "It's for your own good."

Juan managed to get Esmeralda to the Parade, but she wasn't happy.

Hundreds of people had gathered. There were costumes in all colors, and pets of all shapes and sizes.

"Ladies and gentlemen," the announcer called, "time to begin. Keep the dogs away from the cats, and the cats away from the dogs. And remember—don't get behind a horse. Good luck, and have fun!"

The Garcia gang moved forward. Juan pulled Esmeralda along. She shook her head, trying to get rid of the strange leash. "Easy, Essie," Juan ordered. At the corner, he saw Grandpa and waved.

Suddenly, a car backfired. Esmeralda jumped with fright, snapping the leash.

"Stop!" screamed Juan. "Look out! Runaway goat!"

Through the plaza Esmeralda ran. Past the Fiesta dancers, past the snack stand selling Navajo fry bread, past a very surprised policeman.

Esmeralda ran down the alley, knocking over trash cans, scattering newspapers and boxes.

Shaking and snorting, she couldn't rid herself of that leash. Leaping over a rose bush, she landed in a backyard. Straight on she ran, right through the clothes line and around the corner.

"Esmeralda!" screamed Juan, panting and running behind. "Alto! Stop!"

Esmeralda could hear Juan's voice from far down the block. She hopped over a bicycle stand. A car roared toward her and she bounded over the curb. Gathering speed, she also gathered everything in her path — signs, sunglasses, sheets — as she ran up and back through the Parade.

"Stop, Esmeralda, stop!" yelled the children of the Garcia Street neighborhood. Esmeralda skidded into the churchyard. Wham! She knocked over a rummage sale table, sending feathered hats and old handbags flying.

Now she really was trying to stop, but it was too late. Esmeralda, the goat who liked to roam, slid to a halt—right in front of the judges' stand.

Juan and Grandpa both ran up. "Ooh, Essie!" groaned Juan when he saw her. It was a sight wild enough to make him cry. The judge rose slowly and peered over the stand.

"Is this your goat, young man?"

Juan looked over at the Garcia Street gang as they stared in horror. Behind them, Mama and Papa frowned. Juan looked up at the very tall judge. "Yes, sir. This is my Esmeralda."

Esmeralda gazed up at Juan and smiled. Then she nuzzled his hand.

The judge raised the microphone. "For the Most Unusual Costume—the winner is Esmeralda, the goat of Garcia Street!" The crowd clapped as the giant blue ribbon was hung on Esmeralda. The Garcia gang couldn't stop cheering for their winner. And Juan's face beamed as Grandpa gave him a big wink.

Because they both knew...that someday
that goat would be famous.